SA
RY
D0576841

Dear Parents:

Congratulations! Your child is taking the first steps on an exciting journey. The destination? Independent reading!

STEP INTO READING® will help your child get there. The program offers five steps to reading success. Each step includes fun stories and colorful art or photographs. In addition to original fiction and books with favorite characters, there are Step into Reading Non-Fiction Readers, Phonics Readers and Boxed Sets, Sticker Readers, and Comic Readers—a complete literacy program with something to interest every child.

Learning to Read, Step by Step!

Ready to Read **Preschool–Kindergarten**
- big type and easy words • rhyme and rhythm • picture clues

For children who know the alphabet and are eager to begin reading.

Reading with Help **Preschool–Grade 1**
- basic vocabulary • short sentences • simple stories

For children who recognize familiar words and sound out new words with help.

Reading on Your Own **Grades 1–3**
- engaging characters • easy-to-follow plots • popular topics

For children who are ready to read on their own.

Reading Paragraphs **Grades 2–3**
- challenging vocabulary • short paragraphs • exciting stories

For newly independent readers who read simple sentences with confidence.

Ready for Chapters **Grades 2–4**
- chapters • longer paragraphs • full-color art

For children who want to take the plunge into chapter books but still like colorful pictures.

STEP INTO READING® is designed to give every child a successful reading experience. The grade levels are only guides; children will progress through the steps at their own speed, developing confidence in their reading.

Remember, a lifetime love of reading starts with a single step!

Published in the United States by Random House Children's Books, a division of Penguin Random House LLC, 1745 Broadway, New York, NY 10019, and in Canada by Random House of Canada, a division of Penguin Random House Ltd., Toronto. Nickelodeon, Teenage Mutant Ninja Turtles, and all related titles, logos, and characters are trademarks of Viacom International Inc. and Viacom Overseas Holdings C.V. Based on characters created by Peter Laird and Kevin Eastman.

Step into Reading, Random House, and the Random House colophon are registered trademarks of Penguin Random House LLC.

Visit us on the Web!
StepIntoReading.com
randomhousekids.com

Educators and librarians, for a variety of teaching tools, visit us at RHTeachersLibrarians.com

ISBN 978-0-553-52286-0 (trade) — ISBN 978-0-553-52287-7 (lib. bdg.)

Printed in the United States of America 10 9 8 7 6 5 4 3 2 1

STEP INTO READING®

nickelodeon

TEENAGE MUTANT NINJA TURTLES

ALIEN ATTACK!

by Hollis James
illustrated by Patrick Spaziante

Based on the teleplay "The Moons of Thalos 3" by John Shirley

Random House New York

The Turtles are
on a spaceship.

The Fugitoid flies
the ship.
An alarm starts flashing!

Triceratons attack!
They fire at
the Turtles' ship!

BAM!
The ship is hit!

The Turtles' ship crashes on a strange planet.

The planet is cold.
It is covered with ice.

The Turtles are okay.
But their ship is not.

Donnie and Fugitoid
see a hole
in the ship.
“We need metal!”
says Donnie.

The Turtles
look for metal.
Donnie points.
“This way!”

The planet is icy.
Mikey likes to skate.
Booyakasha!

The Turtles are not alone.
An alien attacks!

The alien is
a strong fighter!

Mikey is hit!

He falls.

An Ice Dragon attacks!
Raph and the alien
fight it together.

Raph beats
the Ice Dragon.

Raph and the alien become friends.
Her name is Mona Lisa.

Donnie uses the metal
to fix their ship.

Donnie falls
into a hole.
He finds metal!

Raph likes Mona Lisa.
They promise
to meet again.

The Turtles blast off!

Turtle power!